A TALE OF 2 LOVE STORIES

AS THE TITLE SUGGESTED, WE ARE GOING TO DISCUSS 2 LOVE STORIES IN 2 DIFFERENT WORLDS, AND NOW, LET'S BEGIN

…

VIAAN DESHMUKH SHARMA(V4VIAAN)

Number 1: Space Crush

It was a week before the space programme, and It was the last and most important training of my life, and I was up early.... because I couldn't sleep all night. The training was for 09:00 hours and I was up from 02:00 hours, studying and restudying everything that we had learnt ... 12 times. Fortunately I grew coffee beans. Unfortunately a year's supply was used. I rushed to NASA but my car didn't start. I walked on foot but the pedestrians were filled and with just a little bit of my luck I fell into a pothole. Luckily it was one of the underground tunnels we had practised in during the NASA training days.

I always carried my map in my back pocket and it led me directly to NASA, but since I had packed my bags so hastily, I forgot my map and my sense of direction. I was floating like an astronaut (like in training), navigating my way through this so-called underground tunnel system which in reality is a sewer (the community needs to seriously check the shit). Yes, you can close your nose too, cause I had to close my nose and swim across it, with perfectly synchronised beats (yeah yeah just like in the training).

When I reached NASA, the training was already over, however there was a girl, who was staring at me with a smirk and said "You're late, Mr. Jonathan." As she kept on talking, she noticed I was a wreck and not so politely asked "Eeks, where have you been". I mumbled nervously

"Nowhere , Ms.Veer as I read her name tag on her shirt. I blushed and said, "Err ... Looks like I gotta skedaddle ".

I almost got embarrassed by Ms.Veer, I mean who has Veer for a surname, what does it even mean. Is she Indian, Mexican, alien , who knows , but she's something for sure and that, I can say.

When I came back, She vanished? Poof! so I planned to go home but for some strange reason, I didn't.

I decided to stay at NASA, take a long stroll and maybe even find Ms.Veer, If you know what I mean, unless she's a nocturnal creature. raised my eyebrows in an unfamiliar manner, that even I couldn't comprehend, So I went along with it. After 10 -20 minutes, I saw the office (the place where the people get the council to go to space.)I heard them saying"So, looks like we're down to our final three cadets, Ms.Veer, Mr.Jonathan and Mr.Allison."Another voice said " There only supposed to be two cadets."Another voice interrupted" Well, I say there should be

a competition and the best two cadets should be chosen to go to Space." The main person in charge said "Then it is settled, next week, there will be a competition." I quietly shook in awe and confusion and ran as fast as I could so nobody could spot me.

It was too dark for me to see, and I couldn't use a flashlight otherwise I'd be caught red-handed exiting the spotlight.

Once again I took the first step out of NASA, I fell into my underground tunnels .... again. This time I fortunately had the map. I read the directions, and followed it through, but as night was approaching it was a bit more challenging. In the path there were some scorpions, which tested my fighting and timing skills. And don't even know how but the swamp was filled with crocodiles, which helped in expecting the unexpected.

When I came out , I was swamped, literally and "literally". I reached home drenched and cold (More like sewer cold).

The first step couldn't be sweeter. I took a steaming (and I mean steaming) hot shower. Enough to burn my crocodile's skin, but I needed it , because the sewer is thicker than skin. As I stepped out and put on some clothes I started thinking "How do I prepare for an astronaut competition, which is next week and with no place to train ". That thought repeated in my head a billion times, until I remembered how hard it was for me to travel through the underground tunnels everyday and yet I did it . Maybe, I could use that as a place to train. I went back outside to feel my pride, and once again I fell into the tunnel.

I dodged and fought the living obstacles again, but what do I see this time ... aha, Ms.Veer was fighting them as well. Wait, what is she doing in my spot? How did she know?

Was she following me? Ah so many questions in my head and all I did was begin fighting along with her. She asked me with a loud yell what I was doing while whacking a scorpion, and without hesitating I shouted the exact same as I was punching a crocodile's eye.

Together we replied "Training !!!" and gathered in an outer circle and started attacking. I held her hand and she jumped and walked-kicked the creatures on their bellies, face and vice-versa. Soon all the creatures fled. Ms.Veer looked at me with a clever smile and said, "Thank you for the company. See you later".

She shot a grappling hook and disappeared into the shadows. Before she disappeared, I felt a strange (kind of funny) feeling.

I came back home (again) but this time I was more careful. Took a quick bath and just sat down.

Just kidding...thanks to the non stop exercise regime I officially have inherited insomnia now and therefore continued indoor-exercising.

The next morning, exhausted from last night's training, I ate a hearty breakfast, and took the same pothole route.

When I reached NASA, I learned it was closed until the next week (the competition) I spotted Mr.Brock (third-cadet). He came towards me and asked "Whatcha doing, loser. Haw-haw, whining and crying?!" So I cleverly told him "Look over there!!! "His full attention quickly shifted, and I went into the tunnels again. When he looked back, I was gone, at least to his eye. He said "Whatever", and pounded away from the area. Inside the tunnel, I had a breath of relief, but to my surprise, Ms.Veer was leaning in one of the very corners. I asked her "Brock." "Brock, she replied."She said "Nice seeing you, Coast clear?". I replied "Yup." She said in a hurry "Nice seeing you again". She shot the same grappling hook device and zoomed out of the location without a trace. As she went, the feeling I had before was even stranger than last time. I thought of going up, but I didn't. One exercise couldn't hurt, right. While I was walking through the path, I tripped on something and became unconscious for an hour. When I woke up and came to my senses, I saw a mouse carrying something. I caught it quite quickly and the thing it was carrying seemed like a little gadget. On a closer look I realised it was a shock device (you put it in a person's pocket and he or she will get electrocuted). Luckily, when the mouse touched it, it was turned off. I carried it along with me for my own safety.Who knows when I might need a little bit of luck myself.

I went back home to practise all my equations. Afterall, what good is a strong person, if he doesn't know all his calculations?

Such questions as v=degree/graffs*2&=______, really added another level to my mental physique. I was practising and revising till dawn , and then the fun began. I smirked as I went out of the house and into the tunnel. "Hello, Ms.Veer". This time to her surprise I appeared behind her but she didn't waste a moment to reply with a clever smile " Nice try, but am I really here?". She disappeared into thin air only to shock my guts by appearing twice. Which meant one was the real Ms.Veer, and one was her clone. I said "Punch a crocodile". Their punches went through the crocodiles (Not as in inside out, as if both the Ms.Veer's were holographic clones). She came out of nowhere, Ms.Veer said "Good work, Now let's fight." She quickly threw a smokeball (a device that expands and covers the room in opaque fog. I thought, "Nice, expect the unexpected". Then all the creatures fled, and she said "Nice knowing and seeing you. I owe you one for saving my hide, I said "You're welcome, Ms.Veer." She said " Just call me Annie." "Okay, Annie." I said.

She zoomed away, and the entire cycle repeated until the competition began, I woke up at the peak of the morning, got ready in my finest attire, and took the pothole thrice this time. I met Ms.Veer the first time or should I say Annie. I said "Hey, Annie." She shushed me and said "Not now, you .. you... whatever you are called. Brock's here." Brock heard us and said "Hubba bubba,what's going on here?" He thumped and rumped toward us, but when he came here, we disappeared to his eye once again. She had a zipline, and we both zoomed up without a trace, like she always does. We got out of the sewer and into NASA for the competition.

And the first challenge is... Wait is that Brock running here drenched in sewer slime. Now I know why it should be called the stinker." I saw Annie covering her face and laughing so hard, it made me happy. The main person glared at us with a mean and scary look and said "Now that you all are here, let us begin, …The Competition of Decision." A scary drumroll played in the background.He continued "First up, The Math Attack, each of you will get 10 minutes to solve 100 quantum physics questions... and your time starts now." he yelled. Such questions as 45%of 534262.93/12938+R=___ really boosted intelligence.That boost helped me solve all the questions in 5 minutes and 2.5 minutes to revise. The remaining time was for thinking and I felt an even stranger feeling than before, and I realised that it was related with Annie. Now I know what the feeling was …but suddenly, a groaning lady yelled "Test's over, give the papers." I gave my papers and so did Annie, but Brock said "Hubba bubba, could a lady like you give a minute." "No."she replied rudely and took the blasted paper anyway.The main person snatched the papers and checked the paper and said "Hmmm…….. and the winners are….. Jonathan and Annie by 100%, unfortunately the loser is….. Brock by 0000.1%." He continued "And now, the next challenge, The Dodge and Lodge. It is an obstacle course, filled with booby traps, such as flamethrowers, swinging axes, yada yada, and now let's begin. Jonathan, you're up first. Let's see what you can do." I figured why it was called Lodge of Dodge, I had to lodge the axes into place, and had to keep dodging the flamethrowers. But I got it done, no problem (if no problem means lots of problems) but I still got it done without any minor or major injuries. Annie dealt with it the same way I did, and with ease. But Brock, dear dear Brock, his pants got chopped off by an axe, and his shirt got burned into ash because of a flamethrower. The main person said "Well, it's clear that Jonathan and Annie are going to space. Because Brock failed indefinitely." We all went out and Brock said "You won't get lucky next time, loser."

It was the day of launch, me and Annie were seated in the rocket, just when the countdown began. A crowd was shouting "T-minus 5, 4, 3, 2, 1 Blast off"!!!!!! After 5-10 minutes, a smooth voice recorded said "You are reaching the anti-gravity zone, hold on to something, ASAP". Suddenly, all the objects started flowing, and after sometime, so were we. But It felt like a romantic dance.... in space. But the rocket just stopped in mid flight. "Seems like an electric surge". Annie said . "Unfortunately, we don't have any tools in space". "Wait, maybe we do," I replied. Remembering the deadly shock device I carried for good luck, I threw it in the engine compartment and said "Geronimo"!!! It continued its journey to the moon and reached it in no time at all. We put on our astronaut suits and I took out the shock device. Annie said "One small step for woman, One giant leap for womankind". She pasted the flag on the moon so hard, not even a sandstorm could break it. She climbed back onto the rocket and set coordinates for home, after I threw the shock device in the engine compartment, once again.

We landed back home. She said "Smart thinking, using the shock device for an electric source". "Thanks" I replied. We were about to go our separate ways, but she came close, held me tight, and kissed me on the lip. And then she whispered "If you told anyone I did this, I'll shove your lips into your gut". My, she is strange, but then she ziplined into the sunset. But this time, I came prepared. I carried my zipline from training and zoomed with her and said "I love you", and Annie replied "Ditto".

The end!!!!!!!!!!!

Number 2:Airport Bliss

"It was time to board flight on A-1123, or me and my girl ain't together and if my name isn't Samuel Greens" I thought to myself. Until I saw the most ravishing woman, and I couldn't help but notice, she was looking at me too.But my girlfriend shook me into my senses.

(Meanwhile)

"It was time to board flight on D-9934, or me and my boyfriend aren't steady and if my name isn't Agatha Kartha" I thought to myself. Until I saw the most handsome man, and I couldn't help but notice, he was looking at me too.But my boyfriend shook me into my senses.

(Back to Samuel)

Anyways, Me and Lindsay(My Girlfriend) started our security checkup, and I saw "Her" yet again.As soon as I shifted my eyes, Lindsay slapped me and complained "What is up with you, Samuel?!Get your head out of the clouds or we're through, you hear me!".I replied "Yes, Darling."I nodded my head in agreement, but something was just calling me to her.

(Again to Agatha)

Anyways, Me and Jacob(My Boyfriend) started our security checkup, and I saw "Him" yet again.As soon as I turned my head, Jacob shook like he really wanted an apple and I was the tree and exclaimed "What happened, darling.You can tell me, I'm your boyfriend" "Right?"he whimpered.I replied "Don't be sad , you'll always be my boyfriend, Jacob, my rough diamond."I told him seductively, but something was just calling me to him.

(To The Boarding Gates: Starring Samuel)

Me and Lindsay were reaching the boarding gates(and hopefully away from "her").but suddenly, guess who I bumped into.Her Again!Our suitcase clashed and opened and the luggage fell into the shape of a heart.I didn't think much of it at first because of the constant waiting of my girlfriend for me to pack the bags but after, it felt very strange, like a flint in my heart.But the feeling left after we(Me and Lindsay)reached the boarding gate for A-1123 and just in time too because the announcer said "This is the final call for flight A-1123, I repeat final call for flight A-1123". Me and my girl stood in the boarding line until we finally reached our seats.

I tried to make Lindsay laugh by saying "Now it looks like both our heads are about to be in the clouds"but didn't even get a giggle. "Stop trying to act like a clown,you clown"she said in a monotone voice.

You wouldn't believe what happened next but I'll tell you anyways

Since I took the window seat, I looked out and saw flight D-9934 and "her" again!(Freaky, I know) .

(To The Boarding Gates: Starring Agatha)

Me and Jacob were reaching the boarding gates(and
hopefully away from "him").but suddenly, guess who I
bumped into.Him Again!Our suitcase clashed and opened
and the luggage fell into the shape of a heart.I suddenly
knew he was the one because I never ignore the signs of
the universe, But I never ignored Jacob's feelings as
well.But then it felt very strange, like a flint in my
heart.But the feeling left after we(Me and Jacob)reached
the boarding gate for D-9934 and just in time too because
the announcer said "This is the final call for flight D-9934,
I repeat final call for flight D-9934". Me and my "rough
diamond" stood in the boarding line until we finally
reached our seats.

I tried to make Jacob laugh by saying "Hello, rough
diamond , time to smoothen you up"and realised it was
wrong as soon as it came out of my mouth. "I-It's Okay,
darling.S-Say Whatever you want "he said in a soft and
scared voice.

You wouldn't believe what happened next but I'll tell you
anyways

Since I took the window seat, I looked out and saw flight
A-1123 and "him" again!(Crazy, I know) .

(The Pit Stop with Samuel)

I finally reached Midvale and I think Lindsay is starting to calm down and I thought "Happy days are here again" and I saw an amazing cafe called "Bliss ".

I decided to check it out cause it had FIVE STAR ratings and treat Lindsay to a date.We took a table with candlelight and a bouquet of roses

And the food was cheap, yet divine .It was the best meal I had ever had since birth and guess who spoiled the mood(HER!!).

I finally stood up and said "Why the f&#king hell are you following me!", but the crazy thing was she said and did the exact same thing?!

(The Pit Stop with Agatha)

I had to go to Midvale cause I had to take another plane from there to reach California and I think Jacob is starting to become bolder and I thought "Happy days are here again" and I saw an amazing cafe called "Bliss ".

I decided to check it out cause it had FIVE STAR ratings and made Jacob treat me to a date.We took a table with candlelight and a bouquet of roses

And the food was cheap, yet divine .It was the best meal I had ever had since birth and guess who spoiled the mood(HIM!!).

I finally stood up and said "Why the f&#king hell are you following me!", but the crazy thing was he said and did the exact same thing?!

(The Get-together(Samuel Style))

Since I and "Her" created a scene in the restaurant Bliss, we were thrown out and my girlfriend dumped me for such crude behaviour.So I decided to know about the chick with me.

I asked "Why did you think I was following you, whoever you are?".She said "First of all, my name is Agatha Kartha and second, because I keep seeing you wherever I go."I said "Don't you think that was just a sheer coincidence?"

She replied "No, because I follow the signs of the universe no, multiverse and think about how the luggage fell into the shape of a heart."I said "Well, now that I think about it, maybe the universe was trying to tell us in the straight-forward way possible that we were meant for each other ".

She exclaimed "Exactly!Now you understand loud and clear".I questioned her "But wait,doesn't that mean we're supposed to be together?".

She stammered "Er... ah... oh,``"Wait, I don't know your name"she used that as an excuse to change the topic.I said "I know that's an excuse, but anyways. My name is Samuel Green".

Then the conversation stopped abruptly when Lindsay was wrapped around a jerk's arm.

(The Get-together(Agatha Style))

Since I and "Him" created a scene in the restaurant Bliss, we were thrown out and my boyfriend dumped me for such crude behaviour.So I decided to know about the hunk with me.

He asked "Why did you think I was following you, whoever you are?".I said "First of all, my name is Agatha Kartha and second, because I keep seeing you wherever I go."He said "Don't you think that was just a sheer coincidence?"

I replied "No, because I follow the signs of the universe no, multiverse and think about how the luggage fell into the shape of a heart." He said"Well, now that I think about it, maybe the universe was trying to tell us in the straight-forward way possible that we were meant for each other ".

I exclaimed "Exactly!Now you understand loud and clear".He questioned me "But wait,doesn't that mean we're supposed to be together?".

I stammered "Er... ah... oh,``"Wait, I don't know your name"I used that as an excuse to change the topic.He said "I know that's an excuse, but anyways. My name is Samuel Green".

Then the conversation stopped abruptly when a man-
stealer was wrapped around Jacob's arm.

(The Happily Ever After)

So Samuel and Agatha tried to get together and the results
were absolutely spectacular! Within ten years, they were
married and had a girl named "Robin". So ever
since,whenever they look back at that day, they kiss and
Robin always has and always will say "Ewwwww!".

The end!!!!!!!!!!!

Contents